To Lie *with* Ursa *in the* Grey Cave

Ashton Thayne
with illustrations by
Cassady Bindrup

ISBN: 978-1-7367762-8-5
Library of Congress Control Number: 2021920458

Edited by Vince Font
Illustrations by Cassady Bindrup
Published by Glass Spider Publishing
www.glassspiderpublishing.com

For Mom,

There is something in this poem that Artemis and a whole lot of other people are looking for.

I'm so lucky to say it is something I was never without.

CONTENTS

i: The Tale of the Wolf

Her eyes in the beating darkness;
New blood acquainted with day.
The girl, firstborn, baseborn
Through the Promethean flesh
Brought to clay by
Another predictable conquest of Zeus,
Of a god, sixth born, high born.

Next, the sun
The nursing of his sister's hands.
These bastard twins without a land.
Oh! The blood of an everted womb! Leto!
Her daughter, this half-girl, wanders away.

Not even full god,
She may not touch a throne,
This little lost girl
Who has never known home.

She is walking the woods on bare stinging feet;
Ignores all the turnoffs to towns and to streets.

Behind, half-forgotten, her brother with mother await
To face the sand dragon,
Scorned Heras' little joke,
Seeing another adulteress caught in her rope.
But a quiver of arrows Hephaestus has stoked.
One clean shot is all the boy needs.
The thrum of intent, the echoing trees.

She startles from the first moon-watched nap of many,
Stomach yearning for food
Though she hasn't any.
Poor girl, blind to the wilds.
Blind to her past and to her brother's ascension.
For he is groomed to pull a piece of the heavens.

The thrum of a bow;
How it thrills her wildlife heart.
Stills the hunger for a spell.
Smiling.
Smiling at the quiet inkling
Of some greater plan.

For brother will claim the sun one day
While she will take the trees and beasts.
For now, though, stumbles beneath the first
While the second stalks its newfound prey:

Artemis.

Not quite child, nor yet quite god or beast.
Little *thing* in clads of strips and rags.
She is whining for a father who will not
show his face.
Oh, Papa! Please, Father! Holy Zeus!
Dear Dad.

When the wolves close in and she has not
much to do
But to fashion her fists with the claws of the
forest floor,
Thorny branches that gouge into her grip,

The sweetness of her open god-blood
How it makes them roar.

Indifferent.
Always indifferent.
Zeus watches this show.
And Hera is laughing again.
At least she's forgiven him.
He catches Aphrodite's eye.
Holds it. Winks.
Not much more to say of men.

Below, Artemis holds her own,
She hasn't much a choice.
She grapples a dog to the ground,
Sinks her teeth through its ear.
The taste for blood is found.
She thrashes the canines bound in her arm,
Kicks at the head of a she-bitch and
Loses a finger—an acceptable loss—
One day to be glad it wasn't her bow hand.

At last, the king is between her knees;
The rest of the pups have drawn back.
Like his mother, holds him by the scruff,
And then she breaks his neck.

"My daughter..."
The words come unbidden to Zeus.
In the woods, the mortal woods, the pups
are tamed.
She cleans the blood from their fur.
Back to their caves they take the girl—
Nay, Alpha! Leader! Sister!

The days are blurs in the thrill of the hunt.
The pumping blood in her veins.
Wash of fjord under paw,
Birds that stop singing when the pack is
below,
Meadow that oozes from last winter's
snow.
She is sinew and bone and the furs of her
conquests,
Now less-girl, more-god, mostly-beast.

Artemis? Artemis?

What is a name when there is none for the
nuzzle of den-mate?
The distinct howl of each particular hunter?
Definition over time of each one of their
scents?

What is a name
When the wild dogs don't need one?

The moon chases their nights
Or it leaves them in darkness;
Winter's meager rabbits clutched between
her teeth.
Strong, gamey scent of one kill, now two,
now four
Elk meat.
No. Not elk.
Creature that runs on four legs and defends
with weapons from skull.
Poor, ugly creature.
Creature that ran too slow.
Artemis howls the victory of her pack.
She is bragging once again.

Forgetting her humanity,
Walking ungainly on two feet.
The initial pain of leaving home and feeling
the ache beneath,
Even as a midwife once again
Does not quite remember that first den:
Her brother's birth,
Her mother's womb.

Yet helps to deliver the spring pups as
though they were her own.

At times she is more god:
Putting powerful wolves in their place,
Showing them that she is pack leader,
Leaving them disgraced.

At times she is more beast:
Rolling in the blood of a kill,
Cooling in a pool,
Scratching up against a tree,
Leaving strong scent marks.

Forgetting her humanity.
Forgetting her humanity.
Forgetting her humanity,
Until one day...
She is scouting on her own,
Far and farther still,
For food's been scarce of late
Since frost gripped the western hills.
And she hears a familiar language
Whistling through the trees.
It is a language from some distant years
Yet a language that she's always feared.

And there he is
Against a tree.
The man.
Her instinct is to take him if she can.

Yet the mystery of nature bows her head.
She pads straight to him,
Bloodlust dead.
His hand moves softly across her jaw
And she is awed
And he is awed.
It takes a lot to awe a god.

"Your time has come, my dear," he says.
"For see, Olympus has found need of thee.
To see you walk abroad as wolf....
Well, I've heard the stories sure enough.

"We've seen your daughter they oft tell me,
She's queen of a pack, she's entropy.
Not quite god and not quite girl.
Nor quite wolf, yet close as can be."

Then he said her name and touched her
again. "Artemis."

Darkly surprised to find it had meaning,
She pulled away from that hand.
Pulled away from the words of that man.
Father. Papa. Holy Zeus. Dad.
And for the first time in an age,
She rose to the height of his chest.

"Oh, but you're just a little tyke,
Unproven to our mountain throne.
And yet, in your eyes,
I see how badly you have worked to find a
home."

Her feet felt odd holding alone.
Her arms felt strange in the air.
Artemis dropped her furs to the ground;
Her father brushed back her hair.
More girl... for a moment...
Momentarily stripped back from the guise
of a beast.
She could recognize the words of his
language
Yet couldn't respond in the least.

"I'll give you test.
I'll let you come home.

But first you must prove yourself to the
throne.
Far to the west is the cave and the lair
Of Callisto. Callisto!
Great. Terrible. Ancient. Bear.

"She will not fear a wolf, my child.
She will not fear a girl.
She doesn't even fear the gods.
Callisto has outgrown all worlds.
And if you kill her, take her heart.
Stop the beating of that bear.
For then will you be raised to Olympian
heights,
Praised as the huntress I know you are.

"For you are not a wolf."
The words were the foulest of blows.
"You're a goddess over men and
Over beast as well.
You are not a wolf."

In desperate pity, she howled
The only language she fully knew.
And as they came to her call,
Zeus, hurling his lightning,

Killed them.
Her pack.
He killed them one and all.

For she would never have left
Unless left to her own.
Omega. Lone wolf.
A word few have ever known.

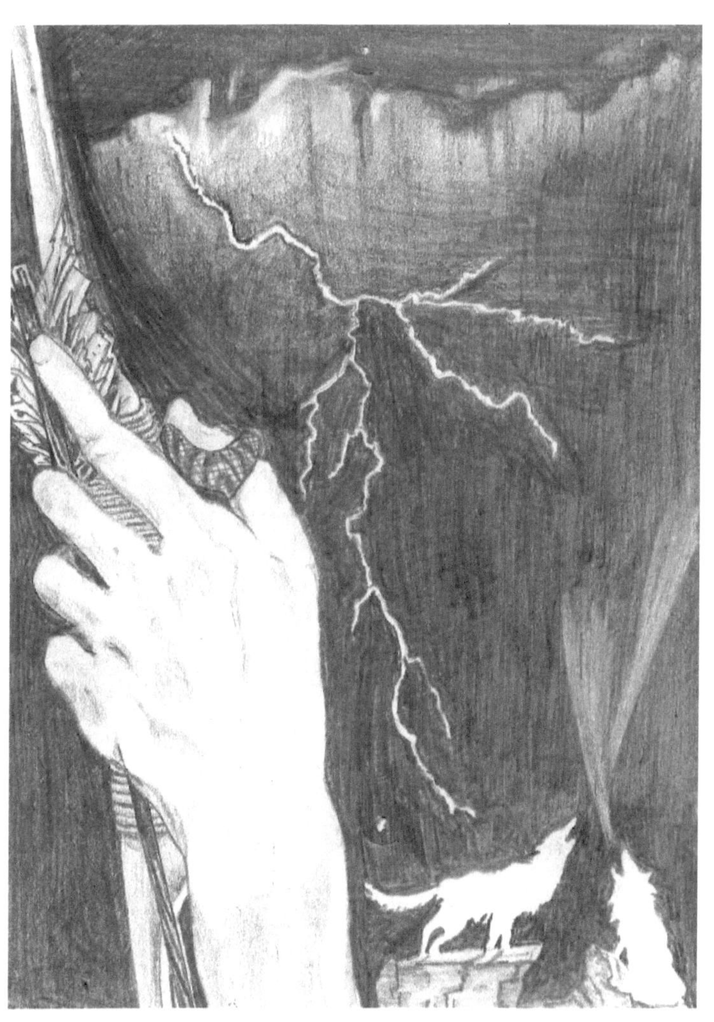

ii: As a Girl in the City

Not a wolf, then.

Only human, only girl.
And so,
She leaves the furs behind and walks
unsteady to a road.
The paved monstrosity, for humans know
no modesty.
Follows and follows it
'Til she enters into city.
Calamity.

Crashing monotony
Of metal beasts that feast on streets
The feces of their strangling smoke
Below these glittering prison walls

Where at last Artemis,
Reflected, can see her face.
Its face.
Still beast.
She startles away from the strange walking
forms
Whose skins are no more than cloth and
paste.

Backward into the round of a bike tire
And honk of horn
With cry of man who yells and
Slams her with his hands,
She runs.
The crash of reeking metal cans,
A backfire engine, clack of shoes, angry
woman.
Shattering shards.
A drunkard's booze.
The fermented air of his cursing.
And new beasts passing overhead,
whirling.

This time she moves without backtrack
'Til the ease of trees
By night their eaves go black.

It's then she sobs,
For she can never go back.

Can never go back
From this maze with walls of brick and
stone,
Glass and bone,
Metal keel, molten steel
And ever-rising chrome.
It is enough to make her shout!
"So where is home? So where is home! So
where is home!?!"

She spent the first night in jail cells
Corralled by men in blues.
Her markings were meant to go in a can,
Not on the floor.
So many rules to not ignore.

At last they forced her into clothes;
A first experience with jeans.
Might as well have been killing her
For the way the young girl screamed.
Then they crammed her in a home with lots
of other girls
Who tried to make an alpha bow

When they had no idea
That she'd been a queen.
She'd teach *them* something!
And soon, everybody knew.

Respect or fear?
It's quite unclear.
The hunt has rules,
And man has not.

But the house of girls was no home at all.
She left it still in the night.
Instead found her peace with the urchins
In the streets
Devoid of those walls adults seem to like.

She learned things then.

What felt like a lot of things.
Some of it useless knowledge,
Some of it essential to her new life
On the streets.
Such as:

Makeup is the blood a wolf would bathe in
But for a girl.

Concealing all the wildness she had left.
Look, now she's domesticated for this
world.
Let her smile at you,
Sneak an apple behind her back.
Now run from the blue men, officers,
Slower than wolves to the attack.
Share the food with starving kids,
These other girls who aren't strong or
quick.
They'd lay down in the mud and die in it
If she didn't take each one and make them
fit into her mold of a new pack.
Hunters, perhaps,
Who didn't know they had a place 'til
Artemis.

Clothes are skins to hide your own skin.
A private thing amongst your own kin.
No more standing naked in the rain,
Basking through summer hurricanes.
Like wolves, at least, boys are the same,
And when they feel the urge to mate,
The boys, they will not hesitate.
A small knife does the trick at least
But clothes help mitigate most beasts.

Food is sparse outside the wilds.
Never once a starving pup,
But often now a starving child.
Dumpsters make for easy pickings.
Don't let cooks catch you digging through their droppings.
Lettuce makes for a weak meal;
Better used as padding against the chill.
Tomatoes are gross.
Starving, eats them just the same.
Each day, no choice, takes handouts
And finds herself more tamed.

The old man.
Wastes whole loaves on feeding ducks
Yet never fails to pluck some off.
The girl's catch is more perfect every day.
Then, with the other girls in tow, she runs to the local market.
Finds the place with free butter,
Her newest discovery as girl.
The bread is then divided, smothered.

Charity: as beast, she didn't believe in it.
Either that or she didn't need it.
On the streets? Another song.

Rarely do meals just come along.
She'd take what she could to beat the odds.
Survive the winters,
Thrive through abuse,
Protect her new little ones.
Safeguard them from Zeus.

Zeus.
He sends his lightning storms sometimes
While she pretends she doesn't mind.
The floods help them discover
An underground line
With one abandoned station to call their own,
Though she doesn't dare
Call it her home.

Artemis grows from what she's forced to know.
Innocent pup once in simple wilds,
Protected all day amongst the whispering trees.
Those days,
Too short.
This one small pocket of humanity
Revokes the child.

In ignorance, she finds her charge bereft,
Cold to the touch with fever left unchecked.
"She's with the golden girl," one says.
All night long they fight against the word:
withdrawal.
But in the morning, she is dead.

In the pockets of a corpse,
Old and torn,
Are all the trinkets of a life
Alone.
The only things she'd ever owned:
A brass hairpin flecked with rust,
A negative shot that's warped with blues,
One name on a slip of paper, the owner
now forgot.
A coin or two.

The following nights are long and loud.
Trashcan fires,
Muttered words,
Sirens singing crime or loss.
Artemis wakes with bloodshot eyes.
Watered-down coffee from a soup kitchen.
Reminding herself, "At least it's hot."

Then trips and spills it up the front
Of a scream.
The clawing of nails in her cheeks
And the stink
Of the newcomer.
Artemis laughs at her face,
A fast way to make new friends,
Then elbows the girl's stomach, sees
yesterday's lunch.
Invites the girl to stay.
Likes any girl what can take a punch.

Payment
Are the words the girl can teach
To Artemis, who only knows the speech,
And of that, just the
Swilling,
Spitting,
Swearing.
Slang learned off the streets.
They start with billboards,
Move on to obituaries.

In a city where there's so much death,
At least one girl is finding joy from all the
loss,

Finding she can recognize these and those
Words.
Laughs and claps!
Even though these are the words Hades
employs
To tell a city he has deceased
Twenty more inhabitants from our
overcrowded streets.

Next week finds her in a library.
She asks for a pen,
Attempts to write something
For her girl that passed.
Eventually throws the tool,
Admits defeat,
No longer knows what she believes.
Goes back to obituaries; just reading them.

Whisper a name
Of a loved one who's passed
Into the black afterlife
Which beyond has amassed
In our heads through ideas and teachings
and hopes,
And that name that you whisper
Has probably crossed her lips.

Crossed at least once

During the next three years she reads them.

Girls come and go.
Some stay.
Others fall victim to the city
And pass away.

They have to leave these bodies in the
streets
Because the issue of police.
Their questions,
Setups,
Drugs that weren't hers or hers to begin
with.
For the homeless are the perfect fallbacks
With no witnesses,
And cops know that judges like
Easy verdicts.

Who cares about the addicts
Now that they're convicts?
Pinpricks.
Worthless little products
Of sexual production.

Parents should'a used a contraception.
No longer human,
Just facts, figures, numbers
On a checklist spreadsheet.

Keep them imprisoned.
Taxes for a failing system.
Privatization.
Illegal citizens.
Fuck recidivism.

In and out of the system.
Can't get a job 'cause you have to show
'em.
Another man suggests he'd be an employer
For an hour
So that he could enjoy her.

At least prison was easier.
Free of these men looking for false
enjoyment,
One short moment
Before sudden exhaustion.

The more that they want it,
The more she takes caution

To guard what
By now a wolf would have taken,
Smelling her god-blood
And wanting her broken.
No longer a queen
Just another possession.

But could rape
Really be worse than the
Weight
Of this city?
Of the high-heeled fake ladies
Who look on with pity?
Or her girls who keep dying,
Or being imprisoned,
Or the trash that they share
With the rodents?
Then at least she'd make money.

And takes the employment,
Giving men their enjoyment.
One rapturous moment,
Then lying there, spent,
She strings bead necklaces 'til they're ready to stand
Or ready to go again.

Sometimes they sit together and smoke,
Which is smart because a kiss costs more than a poke,
And the second time 'round most men want both.

A solid year passes in sex and in hate
While slowly she pays for each girl to fly away.
Wherever they choose, she will pay their cost.
She can take the abuse,
She can handle this cross.
And after a time, it's so easy, you see.
The pain goes away, then so do her pleas.
No more moans while work is in session.
No more panting or thoughts of dissension.
They take her and take her and take her.
She has no exceptions.

Forgets who she was.
Forgets Zeus and heaven.

'Til a wolf walks in.
He is all hair and all teeth.
His breath is foul

With the smell of his kills.
She can tell all he wants is
The taste of fresh meat.

She doesn't scream
As he enters inside her,
Claws at her back
But does not get a word.
Gets angrier and angrier,
The roughest of riders,
But cannot break her iron will.

Still
Rams her up against the bed frame,
Yanks her hair and looks for pain.
Not a word or shout of terror.
And he cannot help but tremor.
Wants to cut her,
Wants to kill her.
Tame this slut who thinks she's
Stronger
Than a man.
One who's holding a gun to her head.

Grabs at it and
BANG!

He is dead.
She is glad.
And he is dead,
And sirens are ringing in the black.
This time, prison will not spit her back.
No more girls to save and
No reason to stay
So at last

Leaves the city.
Hides by day.
Travels by night
Without delay
To the forest
Where first she lost her way.

In it, crumbles to her knees
Beneath the trees
Where someone... someone
Had once told her something.

Made an offer she just hadn't liked.
Hurt her friends...
Flashes of light?
Bolts of lightning.
Smell of burnt fur.

"Zeus!" she yells,
Beating the ground,
Then screams,
"You win! I'm yours!"

iii: The Legend of Artemis & Actaeon

Curling and uncurling,
Unfurling then furling:
The wind in the trees, it lashes the leaves,
'Gainst branches it heaves;
Like thieves in the dark bares naked the
eaves
As she rests beneath.

The swirling of red, yellow, browns of
Autumnal rest
That transports each away
To sleep in themselves
'Til the pale light of day.
'Til they're much like the girl
Curling into the ground,
Sleeps through the night, then,

Opens her eyes, unsurprised.
She has drowned
In the mulch that abounds.

Head up, wide awake, sees the dawn, looks around.

No, not dawn.
She sees pale moon on snow
Falling against the wind.
It is cold that she knows,
And she howls at the cold.

Zeus has not come.
Had he e'r come before?
Or had she just made him up
Once invented his form?
In child pretended
One man could wield such a storm.
The dust settling around her
Is so soft and so warm.

It is blanket and dream
And all the children's books
Which she stole from the library;
Only intended to look.

It is vision in white,
Transporting, not numb.
Where thickest drapes the winter fog,
Is form which draws its dress anew
To curtsy to the little fawn and
Sprinkle footsteps in a dance
That warms and jilts the watcher on.

'Til in a dip of merriment is clearest yet;
A lady in white who drags this veil.
Who could she be?
Artemis knows, and yet...
Still fair and unaged, it is a pale, half-
remembered face.
Shining, dancing, leaping, full with day.
Blossoms catch among her braids.
Artemis reaches out to touch her, hold her,
Tell her how she's missed her.
In tears repent of all the years upon this
globe.
How impossible to live without a mother!

'Til shadow falls and blocks the light,
And then the fateful change.
It's too late to back away

Before
It is a bear.

Then claws! One slash of black.
A coal wept free of light,
Wick of unlit candle in deepest night,
Smoke and ebony and olives on a tree,
The starless sky midst tameless sea.

And no way to escape the slap
That casts her to her stomach upon the
floor.
She screams and feels the hot-wet blood
While the bear just roars and roars.

"Zeus!" she cries into the skies,
But no surprise, he is not there.
It's only girl
And only bear.

He presses again before she's quite aware.
Against her clothes, its claws,
They trip and tear.
'Til gone is the girl, no more in her guise,
Subject to the snow

And those dark, beady eyes.
She is lying down naked,
Bloody and bruised.
Wondering why she can't seem to win
Only fight just to lose.

Which is when she thinks
To discard the rules.
Give up the laws that men have made,
These binds which too long
Have been keeping her tamed.
Instead to bite and claw and growl
And to reclaim
Days when in these woods an alpha fought and killed,
And in that blood had bathed.

She snapped.
Forgot her regained humanity.
And changed,
Unchained.

Dug her claws into those pitted eyes,
Then ripped them out and tried to rise
Against the pitching, rolling weight.
Pulled up a rock and used its shape

To shove it deep into his forest furs,
Perhaps to break a rib or two
Within that pelt that carried
So many smells.
He fell.
He briefly fell.

A spell enough for her to kick and squirm
'Til she had pulled away
To strike!
Fast, without a thought, the tree branch
down upon its angry maw.
He yelled and thrashed, but blind,
He could not find,
And with a final roar, he turned to run.

Then, leaping aft,
'gain swung her mast and
Kept him 'tween the trees.
Beat down, then dodged, with no remorse
As by the wolf she regained claws.
Roared and danced in fall of snow;
Too soon, the cliff, his back was to it.
He lay, displayed, for the earn'ed blow
And by nature's way,
The prince he gave his life away.

Artemis howled her wolf call long thought
dead.
She felt the god-blood rise inside,
Its Aries warmth to quick her tide
Of war upon the huddled mass:
A trophy by the rules of hunt,
Her turn to prove heroic deeds
Or reclaim those broken symbols of
virginity.
Oh, strike this beast! Now best your foe!
The red-hot glory of the killing blow.

Down!
Down hard!

Upon the filthy sheets of once defeat,
So many swords that had kept her trapped
beneath
'Til gone was howl of victory,
Replaced by howl of grief.
Artemis.

She threw her claws and embraced the
bear—
No, did not care about those teeth.
Instead by her grace the broken prince,

His deeds reprieved.

He takes this chance to make his leave.

Artemis, then,
First to a deer surrounded by crows;
Left dead in the wake of the bear.
Removes what remains with tooth and with
claw
To clad herself in the richest furs and tie
them straight with coils of hair.
Feet, legs, a deer pelt hood for her head.
No time against the drawing cold to care
About the smell, about the blood, about the
growing distance
Between her and the bear.

She takes pursuit against her sense, against
the ice,
Follows his trail of cliff down to the floor.
Has no idea where else to go.
Dressed with her thoughts and with the
furs
Then forges on without much rest.
Running footfalls, pounding heartbeat,
Every moment recapturing her once-

familiar beast.

On foot, the days draw into weeks.

Sweating shadow from its backside,
The mountain
Across one moon and to the next,
Rarely sunlight touching down
Upon the faces of the bear
And of the wolf
That travel west.

Deepest shadows call the herds up
Higher to their hidden holds,
And while the ice sticks thick and
treacherous,
The wolf lies down among their fold.
Still and willing not to scare them,
Draws her sorrows to her shoulder,
Smiles and sings to make them know her,
'Til she is elk and she is mother; she is both
a friend and daughter;
Nurses their wounds and treats them to
laughter.

The younger bucks are prideful little

creatures.
They charge and buck and try to woo her
Though know quite well she will not linger,
For by each dawn she leaves to roam
To find her prey and follow onward.
Brother Apollo soon falls skyward.

Such hassle each day,
Hunting for the aging tracks
Of a bear who forges blindly on ahead
toward deeper winter.
'Til there, in the snow, she sees the divots
glint and cover
Miles more westward toward the thinning
Line of blue
Which has been growing,
Still so far-off when there's no knowing
Where a blind bear thinks he's going.
Follows anyway because Artemis has
nothing left except this hoping.

Drifting.
Thoughts drifting.
Days shifting and stars changing, scents all
around.
Mulch, wilting, water flowing, melting,

shelf that's sliding.
Birds are crying, diving, weaving little nests
from strings of hair
That age and, wind-plucked, drive from off
her skull.
Little hints of Artemis, whereon the eggs
are laid with love
In trees with bark that's thickening,
broadening, aching winter off in glorious
Sun-drenched mornings.

A baby fox without a mother,
The panic driving deep inside her,
Which finds the deepest relief
At the loudest hissing sign of danger.
Becoming just that, its mother,
Who catches the baby in its teeth
And beats retreat fast from the stranger.

Pinecones bud like little pots
And above their lids, higher still,
Now only spots
Of snow.
While down below, the river grows
torrential,
Mental,

Fish in hordes pound loud and sometimes pop out through the frothing.
It would once have been enough to make her laugh,
But she's since lost her voice from never talking.

Time has passed since she's seen the bear.
Only tracks remain to trick
Her thoughts away from the pain
Of loneliness.
For the mountain's twilight did not grip the hardest,
Nor even coldest,
As those shadows to which
She'd long been beholden.

Tokens of a human world and world of beast alike,
Traces of her aging face and days ago when she had been a child.
Friends also: girls in the city and the wolves she had raised from pups,
And the wondering ache of, "Where have they gone?"
By night these thoughts would keep her up.

Staring at a moon that held no answers.
Bathing in the river and seeing she'd gotten thinner.
Berries for breakfast.
Fish for dinner.
With the pale glass beating down upon her.
"Where have they gone?
And where is home?
And where is home?
And where is home?"
Footfalls for miles the next day,
Aimlessly following a trail that promises...
Something other.
Something better.
Something... somewhere...
If she ever gets there.

There had been a boy,
He'd lived across the street
And he would watch down through her window
As she'd take men to the sheets.
So much younger than her, barely past his first shave,
Eyes thick with worry whenever she caught him watching,

Though surprised when she was never enraged.
Looking up into his bedroom when he was gone and she alone.
Great canvases had been pressed to the sheetrock with drawings of
Some girl from long ago.

In the reflection interrupted by the backs of fish, some girl.
Some girl who had once been sensual and supple and full.
Thick around the edges, tight between the eyes.
Some girl with a deep, longing expression for a belonging
That is nowhere to be found.
Some girl captured in oil or water or charcoal,
Naked and brilliant and broken and old
And frightened and confident and shallow.
Some girl driven away by the fear of prison
To search the spine of this mountain for
Some other purpose that still seemed hidden.

Some girl who did not exist anymore
Except at a distance.

Stumbling beneath the trees,
Tasting the salt in the air, yet
Unable to find the sea.
Hands bloodied from the branches.
Face pasted with all the mud and blood of being wild.
Artemis begs the land to once again show her a trail.
While knowing, *knowing*,
As beast, she's once more failed.

Tracks lead around in many places;
Scents mingle thick and foul.
The air is polluted by the greatness of the bear,
A scent so dense he can't be found.
Under her stumbling gait, she cracks bones painted tan.
There is no mistaking them for what they are, or were:
Bleached relics of a man.

Artemis has entered a crescent valley

opening to the sea
To find the first bones of many along her path,
Though miles still stretch far and between
With nothing but silence keeping company.

Stillness.
Nothing.

Not a bird or word from squirrels, nor the bugle of the mating deer.
Only this vast blanket of quiet hanging in the air.
Nor the wind in its watchful whirlings filling the cracks in between
A snapping stick, a honking car, a lover's kiss, a shooting star,
The missingness beside a grave.
Desperately, she begins to pray that any noise might fill it,
This void without sound, without shape.
A world tucked away in some corner and forgotten,
Thick and wet and lush and wild.

And quiet, silent, voiceless, mute,

Miming, hushed, noiseless, mum.
Opening her mouth, she tries, but finds no words
To pull into the frantic calm before

SPLASH!

Erupting river.
Wet with the fevering of orange backs that smack and slap
So violently they startle the watcher with their attack
On her senses.
Seems senseless,
All these fish clamoring backwards up the feature,
In thicker toward the heart of the static wood
And the blinded bear, now suddenly standing,
Slashing at the red and orange 'til at last a salmon sticks.
His jaws slam down before it can wriggle free
And escape up the rushing water toward
The *second* bear—

The beast, the god, the queen.

Lumbering across the ground like an
elephant across its plain,
Her furs bunched thick and white around
the head,
Snow sloughing down upon the ground.
Yet this lumbering without the slightest
footfall,
As though earth parting for each toe,
Each royal step
That fell and fell and fell and fell,
Soundless,
Until the two bears meet face to face and
touch; a glacier melting into mud.

'Til Artemis can no longer watch and bows
her head, hands shaking.

Though even watching ground, the child
Finds the world unhinged.
As though a door, open—opening—
Letting light in upon the little things
That should stay hidden.

Like the birds that suddenly voice their

indignation at the wind
Picking up to drive mist from off the water.
Squirrels all at once darting around her,
Chasing unafraid while an ant crawls hand to elbow.
A deer galloping falls between her paws, no pause,
Clearly having taken stock of the smaller bear,
Or perhaps the god,
Who, noticing Artemis bowed below her open maw,
Extends her jaws and roars:

There, deep within the dell, the dull grey-green of memory.
Artemis tumbles into the past.
Where she is watching the men and their hounds
In this, a now-forgotten hunting party.

Their rifles were raised and hunting knives close,
Their horses neighed in the dark of the trees.
Like any entering to this hidden world,

The near ocean hid from them its breeze.

"Actaeon," called one of the men, "there are
tracks here to be found."
Then, dismounting his beast, their fair
leader bowed,
And with them examined the ground.

Deep bear tracks printed the canvas,
Betrayed by seasons of rain.
Along the game trails were more bones
And tree marks to carve out the way.

He moved to their head, a great hunter,
Quite clear,
Face tensed at the sounds in the deep.
Hands close to his gun, knife held in his
teeth,
Fingers itching to set fire free.
And close at the heels of his horse went the
hounds,
Loyal only to he.
Their noses were flared, their teeth they
were bared,
And they sniffed at each tree and each leaf.

Without warning or motion, no sounds in the black,
From behind came the screaming and blood-smell.
"We are under attack!"
Just a blur of large motion,
The swiping of claws,
Though they slashed long as sabers,
Then gone was the god.

Bleeding thickly against the tree,
Actaeon, he propped his bones.
Around and around his baying hounds
And laughing birds within the woods.

In the clearing before were the corpses of men,
The entire party now gone.
Oh! So many noble therein!
And reflecting, Artemis knew she had seen those bones
When first she had reached that great edge of this land.

Actaeon wept his shouts in the dark
As tree-shadow grew into night.

He bandaged his wounds
And the wounds of his dogs.
Lighted a fire
And swept up his gun.

Torch blazing like eyes, he raged through the wood,
Lighting the trees as he went.
Her tracks were deep with the blood of his kin
As he followed the murderess beast.

There was the pond, just lit from beyond,
Glinting from fires he'd stoked
And deep in the pool was the bathing of muscle
And drifting of red in the bath.
The bear diving deep and cleansing its feet
And its maw and its teeth and its chest
From the stink of the men and the sting of their guns,
From the sacrilege brought to her woods.

Callisto:

On closer inspection,

her mountain entrenched
With the scarring past all of the years,
The craters of sword marks and the
shearing of metal,
Their rifts in her snowy-grey furs.
Through each of these valleys, the wet
blood ran clean
As she rolled and fought with the pond,
And washing away in the light of the moon
There was only a bear to be found.

It splayed on its back and it floated and
laughed.
It wrinkled its ears and it roared at the fun.
And naked like this in its innocence played
With the fish that splashed at its back.

Artemis, too awed by the freedom and
wildness and breach—
Peering into nature unbound—
She did not see Actaeon aim,
His rifle a break in the dark,
As those hound dogs encircled the pond
With their prey only yet to be marked.

Actaeon breathed and calmed his mind,

Fixed point upon the head.
His fingers itched to draw the bead
To claim his desperate revenge.

But the eyes that found him gave pause to the draw,
And the goddess at once ceased her play.
For in those black pools was a different force—
Not a bear's, nor a man's, nor a beast's.

Through the woods he was drawn
From his shelf of a tree
Where he left knife and gun.
Pulled to the pool by her look,
Unable to stop or to run.
For by watching her bathe, the goddess, enraged,
Brought her snout to his face and held gaze.
Then, like a trick of the light
Or a cloud o'er the moon,
She was walking away from the lapse of a man.

In his place stood a deer, confused by its form,

While through trees echoed growls of the
hunt.
The baying,
It rent and it tore and it broke
Through the legs and the chest and the face
and the throat
As the hounds fell upon the leader they'd
known,
The hunter, Actaeon.

And wrenched from this memory
Through the death of the roar in her head,
Artemis once again found herself all alone.

Gone were the fish and the birds and the
god.
Gone were the sounds of the shattering
woods.
She was left on the ground, unclear what
she had seen
But reeling from these things, from all that
had been.
Time had passed in these woods, and the
winter was gone,
And above, summer bred thick and green.

iv: In the Grey Cave

In this hollow of the world,
There is a wolf that hates a girl.

It hates her for the fear that holds them back
From searching through this kingdom 'til
The monster, cornered, runs to lay
Its head inside the hidden cave.

The lair Callisto's, older all, older than the first and fall.
Ancient more than man or beast, this cleft beside the sea,
Long forgotten in the deepness of this reach.

They make their home along the stream,
The wolf and girl who fight within,

And hearing footfalls learned by now
Make escape up in the trees.
They feel them shake from rooted ground.

They feel the old world change and shift
And watch the strangeness of her gift.
Callisto, tall and lumbering;
The very plants grow and retreat.
Blooming. Withering. Bearing.
Fruit falling at her feet.

Callisto unmakes all that grows, or thickens bark
To blunt her claws. And from its black, the forest
Throws. Foes for the bear to beat apart.
She hunts the wild boar within, or tracks
A pack of deer to eat.
The strangest yet is when she lays
Beside the sea
And roars that ancient language.
Then out from in the forest stands:

A princely elk, his crown a band
Of many spears painted pale and nicked from brawls.

The honor clear within his stride.
He shows no want to break or hide
And doesn't fight, and doesn't halt,
For neither fear the way of wood,
And down he lays himself before the god.

Callisto smells his fear and in respect she quicks her kill.
A single bite and he lies still.
The strangeness of this place, her will.

Back to nest the girl retreats,
Fear winning out against her beast.
For how to kill the Queen of Hunt?
When that once vision, hunter Actaeon,
Still threads the very thought.

Along the branches tangle twice
The backs of snakes who break and twist and reignite.
Their love dance is a sight apart,
Entreating eye; betraying heart.
Like everything inside this glade, it is a scene
Too pure to watch.
Their nakedness within her gaze,

The sex, its purity, her watch debauched.

Not knowing why, she shakes the branch,
Her violence cascading deep inside.
They bounce and break and fall apart,
Then tangle through the air,
Then land.
And though they wend their different ways
A trace is left behind.
There, at the farthest point of branch,
Dawn catches skin weaving 'round—
A self now put aside.

Her heart pounding a drum,
Artemis pushes branch along behind.
Scooting forward to a hang,
She traces the scales along the edge.
But against any touch, this cage
Crumples in and then is gone.

For the next two days
She is wandering blind,
Abandons the bear for this far roaming
mind.
In the trees, Artemis watches a silkworm
As it forms a different cage of change for its

home.
And along the sea, she walks for a night,
Collecting the trinkets of sand,
Pawing the hollowed cells around in her palms,
How clever, these vessels they take for a manse.
While back in the wood, even wolves leave themselves
In the clumps where they bedded before.
Artemis ponders their coats,
The shedding she holds—how they change and reshape
For the oncoming cold.

What she finds is this truth:
They abandoned old skin.
Each creature, to change and adapt just to thrive.
They floated from home, or they thickened their scales.
They broke free and spread wing to the sky.
She watches them flit at the plants and the flowers,
The moths and the monarchs around and around.

Then remembers a time
When a child had required
To adapt as a wolf
To survive.

Though solitary is their queen
Within her land,
They make pilgrimage before her shrine.
These other bears;
One prince, the blind, now gone away
toward other woods expanding.
There is a summons borne aloft
Within the air, within the rock.

The water makes its course, its current
strong, and sings to all to come along.
To stand in holy places each, and meditate
on wingless light:
The energy of just a bear.
Of other gods, though sightless stand.
Dear pilgrim, beast or man,
Bowed below his loft of prayer.
There is a He for every land.

Olympus and Jabal Mousa
Or looming over Lake Rakshastal.

Transforming men to please the gods;
transform ourselves to fight ourselves.
Artemis steels her fear and goes to pray,
To bow before the mountain
And adapt her ancient selves away.

There she finds one waiting.
A pig, a wild boar.
Then suddenly, the girl is running at the thrashing tusks
And gores herself upon its horns.

There is a momentary lifting, tearing, thrashing,
'Til her swift hand sinks deep a stone blade;
bloodied rock she'd sharpened.
She hardens. Sky darkens.
Breathes and bleeds and bitter clamping,
Clasping, grasping, gripping, nails stapling.
Yet oddly leaves the wound open,
Blood running.

Reeking up the forest,
Waking up the beasts,
A bear chuffs in the darkness,
Twigs snapping toward the east.

Holding still, inching blade free from her kill.
Another prince is lumbering closer to the hunter,
Unaware of her except the smell along the wind that's carrying.
Blood burying itself inside the earth,
Rust ground,
Pooling, pulling sleep, a deep cooling underneath,
Earth tilting.

And in the trap, two are caught; bait waits, bear walks.
The shape, the paws, the nose, the face.
Suddenly the dinner is standing, startling,
A single claw flashing.
Knife catching and glancing off the thickness of the fur.
Roaring in the blackest harrying of two great lunging paws.
Form standing, weight tossing her aside, world rolling and wrist snapping.
Artemis barely clutching her single weapon through the pain of bone breaking.
Claw sprouting from her other paw, barely

blocking the face bearing down its maw.
Blood spattering, beast and human
messing, mixing,
Morphing into wounded dancing.
Her back against a tree—ducking—claws
stripping shrapnel free.
At his stomach slashing and repeating,
Her chest crushed by the weight of his
single punch.
Ribs cracking.

An advance against the pain is the
adrenaline pumping,
Lending her diving roll the speed of its
motion.
Behind, the smaller oak is snapping and
collapsing, branches choking together.
Left behind, the prince is turning and
snuffling, her blood trail following.
On the battlefield, the final soldiers fall into
their stances,
Shoulders frosted with the aching.

And in the distance, far away within the
deepness, a battle matron roaring.

Callisto feels the fighting wake her woods
with warning.
And the smaller bear is distracted, turning,
Soldier looking toward a master's bidding.
Right in front a single cut from chest to
sternum; victory is beating,
Its howling from her lips, uncurling.
Other wolves across the woods returning
The strangest call both beast and human;
It is a prayer in baying, saying nothing
certain.
Holding and retaining, pitch changing.
Through his throat, the final blow.
The hunt completes, she fells the foe.

Then suddenly humanity recurring, vision
narrowing.
All that's left is girl and trees and bear
collapsing—earth, blood sacrifice, interring.
Wordless.

There is no time to regret his passing.
Artemis binds herself to the task she has
fashioned.
Along the wind, the thickness of her blood,
the boars', the bears'—

She fears the smells' enticing and hurries to honor the death
Through her plan, unfolding.

Rolling him onto his back, she begins tearing at the slice she'd made
Along toward his sternum.
The fur and top layer of skin are tough, not giving.
Her stone dagger is rough and blunted from the past few months of hunting.

From chest to chest along the girth, pulls back the fur 'til touching skin
Then slices this along the middle and opens him to peer within;
Reduces him to join the cycle, and hates each pricking tear,
Yet steeling girl, she urges onward
And pushes through her human fear.

If anything learned from Callisto, it's that the hunt is irrespective
To once-learned human false protections which preach respect to numb consumption.

At least the bears and beasts are honest;
each kill to sate their drive for life.
And driving up into his stomach, the girl
abandons man, embraces wolf,
Finds sternum past the lungs and heart.
Then makes the cut and grips the hardness
to pull the bear out of itself.

She leaves the picking to the hunters,
wolves on every side converging.
They let her slip away with her prize—the
skin—
Though follow to the river, where she
further cleans him.
Cleans herself—not her body, but the pelt.
She washes her claws in the river and she
cleans out her eyes for new sight.
Rolling fur along the mud, she dampens
out her blood and freshens the wilderness.
Water rolls inside her chest and out into the
floating onward,
Sun rising over the sudden black hanging,
Salted with earth and absence of a presence.
Artemis dries out the stench of battle with
the human
Discarding all that she had been.

By night once more falling,
Skin lowering, she crawls within herself,
within the bear,
Becoming what was missing.
Morphing.
Skin shedding.

Snakes twisting and leaving their
weaknesses behind along a tree branch.
The bear around her is heaving inward,
stomach stitching and soon fitting.
Hands testing new weapons in the evening
seeping sunlight
Out into the backdrop ocean.
Bark breaking in glorious slashes of playful
scratching.
Roaring at the elk sensed in the nearby
clearing; hunting.
Stretches her sense of smell, the length of
walking on all fours,
The neck weighing heavy,
Her jaws snapping and unlatching.
Unlatching.
Opening.
Doorway widening.
Entering and entering and entering.

Yet still not quite past the portals
beckoning,
She feels the human fighting to flee this
stirring.
To run dashing from the beast that begs
possession.
Each self must fight each self to reckon
Within the hot, hanging fur of adaptation.

In memories she finds this new fight,
Brief flashes of her human life,
And against the fish she wants to tear and
taste
Is the bitter tang of tenderness she'd known
as girl.
The ones she'd saved and sent away, the
lovers she had spurned,
All the times charity had saved, the
starving which had burned.
It returns and returns and returns.

She cannot close this door behind her; and
confused, the bear can only thrash against
invasion.
Not quite sure it's wild or natured,
Caged by things she *has to* sever.

For surely in that grey cave, Callisto
Will sense any weakness, danger, of the
human strangeness.

It takes abandoning all these thoughts and
emptying her mind to the wild.
A pantheon of smells and sounds; a tick
unreachable in her fur.
Wet paws, mud sticking and drying and
flaking, bugs irritating.
Trees overhead and the sickly sweet of
honey; climbing and gouging.
The split burnt wood of lightning having
struck, tinged with the hiss of raining,
Assaulting the flames that were spreading;
ending at the tuneless river.
Getting thinner toward the ocean,
Spurs of wet along the sand becoming
fingers branching.

Human pounding for the soap
To bathe away this stench encroaching.
Hot showers that had burned her skin.
Rudely awakening.
Door still open.
Cage not trapping.

Lashing it back.
Slashing a deer open.
Blood pooling—skin ripping, meat gushing sweet.
The reek of humanity retreating.
The only true beast not quite part of nature's now disrupted circling.
Artemis. Forgotten and forgetting.
And Zeus not showing his ugly face where that other bear would crunch it off.

The goddess, not quite sure why she's so important,
This smaller bear feels drawn to meet her.
To wander deeper into
The secrets of her warren.
So foreign yet familiar.
A massive huntress that leads all other animals behind her.

Callisto.
Sometimes the birds whisper this name,
and it is the same in every tongue.
It is a name with many meanings.
Yet Artemis is sure the simplest form is interpreted as "mother."

Day by day these bears draw closer.
Rolling in her gut, there is something
traitorous seeking closure.

Beside the river, the catch is caught and
bashed and waiting.
Sudden splashing and Callisto drags her
mountain through the deepest water,
Face-to-face before the fishes, which
Artemis nudges closer to invite they share
them.
And then the larger one is pouncing.
Callisto wants a fight, not veneration.

The mountain is
Intimidating.
But battle thrill
Intoxicating.
Immediately cast aside into the beating
river,
Her hands—not paws—reaching for retreat
inside the folds of...
Callisto rages at an unknown disturbance
and bares her teeth and hurtles
Into just another smaller bear, playing.

For deep within, the human self is silenced.
Banished.
Thoughts of fleeing strangled in the growling.
The two bears bump and play and soak themselves in running.
Old salmon interrupted in their flight of winter coming.
Tossing each other around and around, thick skin easily bruising.
Artemis clearly losing.
Then the echoing laughter of Callisto's acceptance.
At last, they pad back beside the water's edge and share the fish
While lying in a sun-drenched morning.

How much can a bear remember?

Where is memory for those not human?
The dog is tamed and exhibits such memory in exhibition.
Rolling, sitting, fetching—then give the bitch a treat for the memory you've witnessed.
Recognizing owner and growling at the

stranger.
The hound dogs bay and play and eat alongside hunters.
But how much can a bear remember?

Where is memory
And where is thought?
Where is the distinction between instinct,
Between intuition?
One of these is human.
Both of these are human.
Both of these are beast, though one of them is lessened.
And why the starkness of this adaptation?
A bear is not haunted by the past it carries.

In the grey cave they pad together, and this hidden place is given a name.
Of this name, "Home,"
Neither is afraid.
They lay against the rough rock sleeping.
Sometimes against the hiss of sea spray
They curl close together and nip the other's fur for sport.
But each of these times slips happily into the next,

Their only preservation—does a bear
remember?—is the blurring
Of all this time together.
A larger cub,
Its ancient mother.

Finding that they love each other,
But that this new love is not like the other.
There is no burden.
In her head, Artemis turns the thought over
and over,
Unsure where she learned that love is
purchased.
The thought disturbs her, tortured.
Rejected memory betraying rapture,
I discard myself and gain another.
But it's not something she dwells on any
longer.

Out in the woods, the wolves hunt together,
Not for themselves and not for the others
But simply because
This pact is their nature.

Lying in the grey cave,
Love is that simple.

One is a child and one is a mother.

Hibernation stills the hungry thoughts
'Til winter has been slumbered
Into fish-thrashing into sprinting river,
And the fresh baby fawn, which is too small and too slow
To offer fun as sport.
Resorting to hunting their fathers, the two bears wander worriless,
Separate, knowing they'll return in days or weeks
Carrying stories and kills from their adventures.
Loneliness banished by the laughter shared over dinner.

A trek down to the glittering pool where the cold waves hide the imprints
Of their heavy tracks.
And they share stories about the strange shapes
Breaching in the mating season,
Their heavy backs—explosions from a different kingdom.
Poseidon's realm, where they're not

wanted.
For her purview is the crawling land and all its natives.
Callisto leads her smaller cub to stand over insects wandering,
And they watch the ants make and unmake their mountain.
Watch backs heavy with the weight of spoils.
There is something to be learned from their persistent gathering;
Something to be learned from all corners Callisto manages.

Under those great paws of hers, the earth grows and retreats.
Flowers and weeds and saplings,
Salves and poisons.
Narcotic leaves that twist into life then decay.
They reek with euphoric passions.
Induced, the forest gives up its dangers as humors.
The mating elk in their clumsiness,
And the way they fight each other to sustain their bloodline

With a single female.

Then their babes; the thick smell of milk
and blood and weaning;
Awkward stumbling. Shuffling into one
another and competing for mother's teat.
Unwatched, they watch.
Artemis and Callisto.

One follows and sees what the god sees,
While the other sees across
Into every forest,
Feeling every breath of every fortress.
The hunts and dens and spoiling vultures
cawing.
Or the tree trunks breaking in the swinging
metal strangling,
Machine smoke entangling,
A train of chainsaws disturbing birds who
wordless migrate
Toward a secret shelter; the hidden glade of
Callisto's warren.
Untouched, unseen by most—the only
forest of its kind, by man yet unburdened.
Though Artemis sees and hears and feels
none of this;

Devolves back into innocence and forgets
and forgets and forgets.

Culling the herd through hunt.
No more overpopulation.
Days spent herding salmon.
Their guts feeding the soil.
Burned sections refreshing wooded
mansion
And ripping at the blackened bark.
Only a bear can know this much abandon.

And forgets and forgets and forgets.

The blackberries have a sweetest season.
Lying beside Callisto, the grey cave holds
them both.
Winter falling, unending. Little foxes poke
their heads out.
Undisturbed, their bellies stuffed full with
sleeping.
Icicles creeping across the mouth, hiding
this place.
Spring passing, summer lashing its heat
waves into
The two bears diving, fighting, rolling,

splashing.
Never growing tired of the monotony that is really never the same.
Wilderness always changing. Funny squirrels they cannot catch—too quick and small.
New places to collect the sweetest honey, and fresh fruits finding new growth, now discovered.
Dinners shared beside her mother, Callisto.

Forgetting and forgetting and forgetting.

Hunting alone after the charging buck,
Artemis cannot shake the sensation off.
She feels that she is being watched.
Ignoring sense, the bear drives on, is thrilled by her speed,
The propulsion of her many claws,
Of her heart beating in the muscle that is surrounding all around.
Not fat with fur, but a hardened weapon stretching and coming back
Together in a run; in the hunt.
In the leaping and clawing
at the legs of the buck,

Hobbling him—breaking his sprint—about to tear into his throat
When the bear stops and sees the man.
Long beard, bright eyes, old father, darkening sky.

The buck jerks free and breaks her concentration,
Hoof digging in with blinding pain then stumbling away.
She does not care; turns and slashes where she'd seen him.
But there is nothing. She is alone.
Spring is a calm and damp and semi-silent season.

Returning to the grey cave, she does not share this sighting with her mother.
An empty secret draws itself a woven net inside.
She does not eat that night, and by morning feels that burning hunger.
Out hunting once more, she sees a reflection.
An ancient man with his walking stick, washing himself within the water.

Lunging!
She scares up all the fishes, cracks their eggs, scatters rock.
Across, as she reaches, the bed of the river is empty and listless.

For the first time, a bear finds itself haunted.

It sees the old man in the blood of the meat being eaten
And hears him whistling along the seashore.
His ghost snaps branches as it follows,
But nowhere can her claws find purchase.
Thinks to tell Callisto, warn her, yet knows deep down the betrayal certain.

A forgotten self, resurfacing,
Her head splitting heavy under thoughts and emotions.
Imprinted in the bark of a tree, she slashes where she sees his face;
Turns and chases his running boots;
Trips and sees him dancing in the trees;
Is taunted when she starts to climb, and

there is no one to be seen.

In the grey cave, the bear awakes and
panting, stands.
Slams into the wall of the cave.
At night, he infiltrates her dreams.

Zeus.

Callisto stirs but does not wake.
Her royal form rolls, sleep retakes.

The heavy breathing echoing inside the
cave.
And suddenly that Aries war sparks inside.
No more can the human hide.
For there is still that goal prying escape,
To exact the hunt and claim her birthright.

Then the shame; deep shame.
It overpowers the flaming strength and
dampens
The air of the cave.

Memory and past collide.
They revoke the bear her mortal self denies

And replace it with the hanging weight
Upon the slender human shape,
Dragging her down, unnatural,
Taking it all away and replacing it with blinding pain
And shame and rage and pain and shame and rage and pain.

Nothing left to reclaim; the skin is just a disguise
Around the human lie.
Artemis has carried it with her all this time:
The stone dagger at her waist.

Betrayal.

Yet it draws her nonetheless, the strength of this ancient quest
To hunt Callisto—the goddess bear—and take her life.
Title claimed, goddess earned, in tales, her name enshrined with fame.
And it's at her side, the dagger,
And Callisto sleeps there beside the cold grey cave entrapping.
The word that they had called it slipping,

just out of reach.

All the simple words and feelings darting
away.
Bear pelt hanging.
Artemis, as ever, aware that her constant
shape knows this changing.
Knows wolf, knows alpha, knows girl, and
orphan.
Now it even knows bear.
But all of these are mortal instruments.

Deep down, she knows she has never
known herself as goddess.
What is that adaptation?
Untouchable, unhurt by all the mortal
chaos—all the aging that betrays her.
A past that's scored with pain and longing.
And there, sleeping,
The subject of its ending.
For some reason, the hunter finds that she
is weeping.

Had she seen him in those woods? Zeus?
Or deep inside, was it an image
Her mind just kept creating?

Waking the hunter up.
Dagger unsheathing and pulled between the thick skin,
Peeking out between the claws.

Laying her bear-self down once again,
Within the arms, Callisto,
Asleep within the grey cave.
Weapon inching closer.
The only way, she once had found,
To disguise herself and kill this monster.
You do not suspect your kin and partner.

There is the razor, poised before the throat,
And the goddess is unsuspecting.
Cannot confront or change the human
Is fading into myth and legend.
The fatal cut is quick, knows mercy.

Yes, this is when the stars change.

They both die.
Two bears: a mother and a daughter.
In a crack of burning lightning,
The maker is standing there before them.
He is proud—he is her father.

And yet this man is foreign.

Respectful, or so he thinks,
He wakes his will and places hands.
Sheds free the girl, Artemis.
They stand above two broken queens;
The bears, the child and mother,
And Zeus then sets them there together
Up above, outside the cave,
Ursa Major and her minor.

Sailors watch on storm-tossed seas.
They are lost by all the strangeness,
Cannot navigate against stars changing.
But stars do change.
The Fates align themselves.

They dig through the mess of mortal hairs,
Plucking through the aging throng,
Seeing all the deaths that will,
Willing them to wait a while.
At last, the fate of the child,
Still so young
Yet blood so aged by what she's done.

From the mess, the Fates remove this

strand.
Then watching the changing
Of all the human she had left,
Artemis stripped free of this mortality,
Our ever-present weight,
And loosed upon the cosmos of knowing
everything.

Seeing all the chattels 'neath her gaze.
The woods gathering beneath her power.
Taking the beasts from she who once had
been their queen.
Watching them all awaken in their separate
homes,
These girls Artemis had known,
And their race to Mt. Olympus
To recognize her coronation.

They expect her to laugh and smile,
To take and hold her hunters.
They'd known her once to jest and joke,
To challenge them to silly contests.
But they find that she is gone,
The girl they'd known in that city long ago
In the days now parted by age.

For many a year had passed since they had
seen this face.
The strangeness of it, and its familiarity,
And the growing beauty—
Almost unsightly—
As Artemis embraces these powers of
immortality.

"And now, with us, you'll stay," says Zeus.
But he has made a mistake.

A father is surprised to hear his daughter
laughing.
Not in joy, or satisfaction;
Artemis is laughing at him.

At all the silly gods in all their silly robes
In these, their gilded thrones.
They are sitting around this great table of
our world,
Counseling how best to handle all the
realms they hold.

And then turning, Artemis, she says,
"The wilderness will never be yours."

Goddess and her hunters, they take their
leave.
And none can take back the immortality or
strength
Which to Artemis was given.
A bribe to make her kill the Great Bear,
who also wouldn't
Join this pantheon of rule and wisdom,
Or sell the woods—
all these woods.

Artemis now collects them, protects them,
Races through them with her hunters.
They make games and they cook over
roaring fires.

When the men come, they tease and scorn
these liars and betrayers.
They have dalliances with thousands of
lovers
But never sell themselves fully to another;
Only to their queen.

She takes them from country to country
through all the forests of the earth,
And their arrows know every animal that

ever will and ever was.

Nonetheless,
Above the stars reflecting,
Artemis is bathing naked in their shining
brilliance.
Two constellations constant,
Their rhythmic haunting.

Though endless her days,
The Queen of the Hunt,
And great are the woods and the maids
For this god.
She finds herself wandering, haunted
By that one thing she had done.
A secret of nature now lost by her blade.

They feel it sometimes,
The silence of her crime,
And no huntress can comfort
The bear once betrayed.

Their leader leaves them
And wanders for days.
Abandons respect and this power, the crest
of the gods.

They never were home,
It was something she'd lost.

Artemis wishes and wanders, and mourns
What she's gained.
Remembering days when she'd fought and she'd played
As a true wild creature in the glade
Of Callisto.

And she longs to lay.
And she longs to lay.
She lied to the truth of the wild she had found,
Abandoning what had been home
For the weight of this crown.

Now the woods are hers,
And the beasts lie down.
The birds fly south
And the seasons are bound
To the wills of the goddess,
To the whiles of her charm.
To the torrent of rain when she finds
She is still a lost child.

But there is nowhere to sleep,
And no place to call home.
That old den is lost to her mind.
As are the great trees that she still cannot find.
The sea is forgotten,
And so are the smells.
She loses herself in every forest they dwell.
She calls for Callisto, long gone to this world,
And stares sleepless at stars
That stare back at the girl.

And she longs to lay.
And she longs to lay.
To retrace her way to that hidden place.
To clad herself in those furs.
To hunt with her mother and play with the animals.
To rest her head
Safe and sound back at home.

And she longs to lay
And sleep away
These haunted memories.

The fear of losing home, now lost.
The weight of ruling over all that hunts,
And the weight of what it cost.
And she longs to lay and sleep,
Somewhere in the deep of memory
Beside the sleeping bear.
And she longs to lay.
And she longs to lay.
And she longs to lay.

To lie with Ursa in the grey cave.

About the Author

Ashton Thayne Bindrup spent his early childhood learning how to write on a brick laptop handed down father to son since the stone age. Its fan hummed so loudly it would eventually vibrate from table to floor. Inevitably, this is how it—and his first "novels"—met their demise. For his early fiction, this may have been a compassionate act of God.

Not to be deterred, Ashton has continued to write. His poetry prefers pen and paper; he has bought a working laptop for the prose. Today, he is an English major turned freelance writer, turned server, recently turned local restaurant manager. He writes in bursts following late-night shifts, getting out the paragraphs he's been holding in his head all day.

His words have found a home in Ogden, Utah, just down the road from the haunting childhood canyon that first inspired his imagination to seek out a written self. Many of the stanzas in this poem refer back to images from those early years.

Ashton lives in a dysfunctional 1920s apartment with its long-dead ghostly inhabitants, his talented partner, Conner, and their unique dog, who sometimes goes by the name of Fennel.

To Lie with Ursa in the Grey Cave is Ashton's first book of poetry. It is also his first published work.

www.ingramcontent.com/pod-product-compliance
Lightning Source LLC
LaVergne TN
LVHW091011080826
845145LV00003B/1231

* 9 7 8 1 7 3 6 7 7 6 2 8 5 *